MW01680929

KRUSH

Novella

DirtSlap Series #3

By

Ashlynn Pearce

KRUSH

Print Edition

Published by: Whimsy Notions Press, LLC

Cover artist: PickymeArtist.com
Editor: Patricia D. Eddy
Formatting: BB eBooks

ISBN-13: 978-0692424643
ISBN-10: 0692424644

10 9 8 7 6 5 4 3 2 1

Dedication

As always, to my Hubs. I love you.

To my writer girls…
Linda, Nichol, Silver and Jennifer ~ You are the best and always have my back.

Writing Wenches ~ *Ya'll are one awesome writing group and I'm so thankful to be a part of it. You rock!*

To every person who reads my stories.
Thank you.
It's been a long road getting back and I cherish that you've taken the time to buy and read my books.

Love and happy reading/writing!

CHAPTER ONE

ANGEL BRAYSON STOOD on the deck of the cruise ship, but instead of enjoying the view of the never-ending expanse of water, she held her phone to her ear.

"No, Dad, pirates aren't going to hijack the ship."

"I don't know why you had to go off by yourself. You should've stayed home. Matter of fact, go ahead and get off that damn boat and get home where I can keep you safe."

"I am not a kid anymore. I'm twenty-five. I don't need your permission." She shoved her big sunglasses atop her head and pinched the bridge of her nose. "Even if I wanted to, the boat has already left shore."

Not that she got to enjoy that either. She'd been too busy arguing with her dad. She loved him, but he was part of the reason she'd run off on this fourteen-day cruise to start with. She needed a break. From him, from Nashville… from everything.

"You can swim. You can't be that far from

shore yet."

"I'm hanging up, Dad. Love you."

She ended the call, turned off her phone, and released a big pent up breath. She tuned out the people around her and focused on the waves. The salty air tingled on her skin. The sun shone high overhead and warmed her bare shoulders. She shoved her glasses and phone into her black cherry backpack and ambled along the railing.

She'd never been this far from home without family or friends, but wasn't it about time to figure out what *she* wanted to do with her life?

Thrand obviously wasn't it.

The pain was still sharp. Not because she'd lost him—because how could you lose something you never had? But because she'd lost a lot of time waiting for Thrand to open his eyes and see her.

Except he saw someone else.

It was a lot like being dumped over the head with ice water. It left her cold, alone and shivering. Seeing Thrand with his girl, Cassie, and then watching her cousin, Ethan, get engaged was enough to make her scream.

No way in hell was she going to the wedding. Right now, all that mushy shit set off her gag reflex.

What she needed was time away. Fresh air with people she'd never seen in places she'd never been.

SHE WANDERED THE decks aimlessly. The sheer size of the ship staggered her. Like a floating city, she passed everything a girl could ever want. From shopping malls and salons to clubs and bars. She stepped into an elevator and hit Deck Six.

A cruise in June seemed to be a hotbed for a lot of that mushy crap she was trying to avoid. The couple in the elevator were not helping her gag reflex. Nor was the pin the 'bride' wore.

She hurried off, found her room, and pushed into the tiny stateroom. Her bags were already there and she walked around the king bed and then slid open the glass door. She'd splurged and her reward was the small balcony with the ocean view.

Perfect.

She closed her eyes. Just be. Nothing but the sound of the waves reached her ears. She collected all her thoughts and stuffed them in a box. Be. She could reflect later. There was plenty of time. She stretched her arms up over her head, spread her fingers wide, pushed up on tip-toes and breathed.

Let it go.

Her heart beat. Her pulse was light. She opened her mouth and… screamed.

Long.

Loud.

The sound got lost in the waves.

She opened her eyes, laughed, and pushed at

her cropped hair. Ah, yes. Much better. Nothing like a little scream-therapy. It was totally underrated for dealing with daily shit-storms in life. Or in her case, years of stupid.

She turned her attention to her clothes, shook out the wrinkles and hung up her dresses. Mostly black, with splashes of red and white dominated the closet. She picked out one, tugged it on, and slipped on her wedges. Cherry-red lipstick finished off her look before she headed out.

"I'M TELLING YOU, this is made wrong." Angel eyed the bartender and held up the offending drink. It tasted like vitriol and gasoline.

"Lady, that's how I make my drinks. They have bite. People go on cruises to get drunk."

"Probably true and bite is fine. But this is sex-on-the-beach. It's supposed to be fruity. It's for girls." She narrowed her eyes on his nametag. "Donny, I'm a bartender. Best one around. So let me show you how it's made. You'll sell more drinks if they actually taste good."

"You?" The guy looked her up and down and sniggered. "You look more like—"

"Don't say it, punk." She pointed a finger at him, sat on the bartop, swiveled, and plopped down on his side.

"You can't do that," he said.

"Shut up, watch, and learn." She smirked and

poured eight different ingredients into the shaker.

"That is not how you make it. Lady, you're kooky."

"I may be kooky, but these are my specialty. I sell a shit-ton of these." She poured the mixture into a glass and handed it to him. "Try it."

He took a sip. "You can't taste the alcohol."

"That's the point. It hits 'em about number three, depending on how lightweight they are." She hopped back on the bar, turned, and slid back onto her barstool. She stopped the first guy she saw by shoving the drink at him. "Try this."

COLE ROSIN STOPPED just short of running into the drink that was shoved at his chest. His gaze tracked the pale slender arm to a girl. Straight, black hair framed a doll-like face with storm blue eyes and red lips. He raised a brow.

"Why? Is it poisoned?"

Her smile transformed her. Warmth emerged from that porcelain skin and those eyes twinkled with mischief. "I'm bad, but not that bad. But no. I just want to know which you like better. This one," she held up the one in her hand, then pointed at the glass on the bar. "Or that one."

He stepped up to the bar, took the glass and sipped. "A girl drink."

"That doesn't matter. Just tell me if it tastes good."

Her fingernails were painted black, her dress was black with red cherries all over it, and she reminded him of a fifties pin-up. Pale, bare shoulders, and all. Intrigued, he took another drink, rolled it around on his tongue and gave it more thought.

"Yes, it's good. Although, I'm not sure I'm the best judge." She waved a hand for him to drink the other one. He took a sip of it and choked. "Are these supposed to be the same drinks?"

She gave the bartender a cheeky smile and picked up the good drink. "There's your proof. Do it right next time."

She slid off her stool and tilted her head up so those dark blues met his. "Thanks, darlin'."

Her voice trailed up his spine as she sauntered off. A pin-up girl with a southern accent. She had to be the most interesting thing he'd seen in years. As interesting as the large day-of-the-dead girl tattooed on her left shoulder.

"Wait up." He caught up to her, and her dismissive look made him hesitate, but only for a moment. "With an accent like that, I gotta ask where you're from."

Did I really just say that? If he didn't think it would make it worse, he would have smacked his forehead.

She rolled her eyes and twirled the straw in her drink. "Come up with that one all on your own, did ya?"

He shoved his hands into the pockets of his slacks. "Yes. I did. And that was pathetic. I'll slink off now. You have a nice evening."

He turned on his heel and walked away. Nothing like a dose of dumbass to embarrass himself. And he hadn't been embarrassed in years. He raked a thumb across his chin and stepped out onto the deck. Overhead, a million stars greeted him.

He found a quiet part of the ship and leaned his arms over the railing. He should be in his room, going over the plans for the new house he was contracting. Not making a fool of himself and now brooding about it. He'd once been known for his smooth words with the ladies. Not so smooth anymore.

"Nashville," a feminine voice said beside him. "I'm a bartender. So where are you from and what do you do, handsome?"

He grinned and faced her. "Denver, and I'm a contractor. Tell me it wasn't pity that sent you out here."

She gripped the railing behind her and wrinkled her nose. "A lil."

He nodded. "Fair enough. I'm okay with pity."

She laughed and looked up at the night.

"Gosh, the sky is big here."

Her skin was almost luminescent in the darkness, but he tore his gaze away and looked up with her. "Same night sky you see every day at home. And everyone sees the same sky. The only difference is perception."

"Ah, but that's the tricky part. Perception can be such a bitch."

"Very true. I'm sure your perception of me is a poor one."

She slanted her eyes at him. "It's improving."

"Since cliché lines are my mantra, is this your first cruise."

"It is. First time I've needed a passport, and it's long overdue." A somber expression settled across her face. It bothered him. She had a smile that lit up her eyes.

"My family has been on many cruises. You might say they have a travel fetish. I know all the good places to see away from most of the touristy traps. We'll be in Grand Turk tomorrow. Would you like to go ashore with me?"

Her red lips quirked. "You're not a pirate, are you?"

"Pirate?" He laughed. "No. Is that a problem?"

"My dad was sure the boat would be hijacked by pirates. And Dad also said not to go anywhere with strangers, and since I don't know your name..." Her shoulder came up in a shrug. "I guess I'll have to say no."

"Your dad is a wise man." He stuck out his hand. "Cole Rosin. And you are?"

She slid her hand into his, and a shock prickled up his arm and the back of his neck. Her eyes widened and her lips parted.

"Angel," she said in hushed tones. "Angel Brayson."

Her small, pale hand fit nicely into his. He reveled in its softness against his calloused one. Awareness spread through him. A new sensation. Something he'd never experienced. It left him unsettled, unsure, because he read the same surprise in her eyes.

She pulled her hand from his, put it on her hip, and took a step back. She tilted her head so the moonlight highlighted the angles of her face. "Have we met before?"

He shook his head and curled his hand to keep her warmth there. "No. I'm positive I would have remembered."

Her brows furrowed, and warring thoughts flickered across her face. Had they not touched, he was sure she would have agreed. But there was something in that touch.

He felt it.

He was sure she did too because her retreat had been immediate.

"Angel," he said and relaxed his stance. "I have

no hidden agenda."

She arched a brow. "Are you trying to assure me you have no intention of trying to get in my panties?"

Her blunt speech made him choke. "I guess, in my polite way, yes, that's exactly what I'm trying to say."

Her flirty smile was back, along with the twinkle in her eye. "All right. Since you seem so sincere."

She pulled an extremely colorful phone from the pocket of her dress and handed it to him. "Put in your number. In case I change my mind."

He took it, punched in his number, and shook his head. "You plan on ditching me?"

"Not necessarily. But before I go... you said you were from Denver, yet you have a lilt to your voice. An accent."

"You are very suspicious," he said and handed back her phone.

"Matter of fact, I am. So instead of wondering, I just ask, then I can mull over whether or not you're lying."

He barked out a laugh. "As I said, my parents loved to travel. I was born in Rio De Janeiro. I speak Portuguese and Spanish fluently. That is what you're hearing."

She tapped her phone against her chin, obviously weighing his words. "Plausible."

"So what could be your hidden agenda?" He decided to turn the tables. This verbal sparring was as refreshing as it was exasperating. He wasn't used to being questioned. In his world, his word was taken as fact. He crossed his arms over his chest and smirked.

"I have none." Her big eyes stared up at him, but he couldn't read them. Partly because he didn't know her, but mostly because he was sure she didn't want him to read her.

"See you tomorrow, Cole," she said as she turned and walked away.

He looked down at his hand and opened it. Her warmth was already gone, but the tingle she'd created lingered. He rubbed the center of his palm with this thumb. It had been two years since his wife died and he hadn't been a saint.

Yet no one had ever left such a quiver of awareness.

A stranger named Angel.

He looked up at the empty space she had occupied. He had the rest of the cruise to figure out what that sensation meant, if anything.

CHAPTER TWO

ANGEL MADE IT to her stateroom and leaned against the closed door. Her breath hitched, her pulse pounded, and she was totally thrown off. Who knew handing someone a drink would end up so… nerve-wracking?

One thing for sure, she had never felt *that* with Thrand.

She'd been friends with Thrand for years. Hugged him, hung out with him, talked and laughed with him, and never did she feel *that.*

She didn't even know what to call *that.*

She tossed her phone on the bed and eyed it like a leper. She'd met all sorts in her line of work, from the drop-dead gorgeous, to rednecks with a beer guts, to bad-ass bikers. Looks meant nothing, and despite his clichéd line, Cole was smooth, polished, and heaven help her, that accent. She put her hand to her head.

All she did was shake his damn hand and—*that*—zinged all the way to her toes.

She was trying to get over one relationship—no, that wasn't right. There had never been a relationship. She stomped over to her art bag, pulled out her sketchpad, and flipped it open. A drawing of Thrand stared back at her. All tough and hard with his cocky grin and she felt… nothing.

She flipped page after page of images of him sitting, talking, drinking, playing his drums—she dropped the pad like a hot rock.

"Fuckin' A."

What did any of it mean? How could she go from heartbroken to nothing in a flash? Was she really that shallow? Had all this time pining over him been something she'd built up in her head? A simple teenage crush she'd let take over her life?

Indecision had her torn, so she left the decision alone and met Cole on deck the next day. She hid behind her sunglasses and took him in. Tall and dark, he had hair that made her want to run her hands through it and lips that should be illegal on a man. Full and tempting and right now they were smiling at her. A crooked, one-dimple smile. His style was simple—a fitted white tee with khaki shorts. Yet somehow he blared class.

"Good morning, Angel. So happy you decided to join me."

She stopped in front of him and tamped down the urge to melt at the sound of his voice. "It was with serious thought. But I do have a condition."

"A condition?" His golden eyes crinkled. "I am

not surprised. So what is this condition?"

"We stay in the popular areas. I don't need to deal with a kidnapping or something. Messy thing when it happens in a foreign country, so I've heard."

His brows shot up and amusement danced in his eyes. "Your dad?"

She smiled. At least the man had a sense of humor. "You got it."

"As her father and the lady wishes."

THE ISLAND WAS beautiful with its white sand and bright blue water. The man lived up to his word and didn't press his luck or make any advances toward her. She could almost say he was overly polite as he led her around the island. Like her own personal guide, he knew more about the place than the official tours.

He chose the place to eat for lunch and then ordered for her in Spanish.

"Show off," she muttered.

He gave her a grin. "Tell me, Angel, how did you come by such a name?"

She sat back and huffed. "Another cliché line?"

He looked down, then met her gaze. "Yes, I'm sure you have heard that line many times, but I am genuinely curious."

She regarded the sincerity on his face. "My dad. When I was born, he called me his perfect lil angel and it stuck. They did have other, better, names picked out, but for some God-awful reason, decided to go with this one."

"You don't like it?"

"You're really asking me that?" When all he did was raise his brows, she laughed. "I'm completely aware how people perceive me. Then I tell them my name and it's like a double whammy. Invariably, it isn't long and I get the 'are you a stripper' question."

He looked appalled. She still couldn't decide his angle. And even though he said he didn't have one, she knew that for a lie. Everyone had an angle. It was just a matter of time before he revealed it.

"Tell me something about you." That was enough about herself, and she popped a piece of grilled shrimp in her mouth.

He wiped the corner of his lips with a napkin and laid it on the table. "What would you like to know?"

"You don't want to talk about yourself." She lifted her chin, catching on to his hedging.

"You don't miss much, do you?" He leaned forward and laced his hands together. "I'm from a large family. I have three brothers and two sisters and we are all very close."

"But?"

"But, what?"

"I can hear it in your voice."

"But they are meddlesome." He took a sip of his Corona. "I'm starting to think you are as well."

"Only to those who seem to be hiding something."

COLE TILTED HIS head back and laughed. "Do you always say what's on your mind?"

"Almost always." Her black hair was stark against the white wicker chair and thankfully, she'd taken off her shades. He liked watching the play of light in her eyes.

"Good. Don't lose that."

She dipped her chin and looked him square on. "So what are you hiding?"

"Nothing." Not exactly a lie but it wasn't exactly the truth either. "You ready to see more?"

"Sure."

They walked outside, and when she was about to step into the road, he pulled her back as a moped sped by, barely missing her. With her back pressed to his front, he heard her sharp inhale. The top of her head stopped just below his chin so when she looked up, her lips were inches from his.

"Thank you," she murmured.

He released her, stepped back, and puzzled on the way his body reacted so strongly to hers. She wasn't his normal type. Neither tan, tall, nor long-haired, she was the exact opposite of every woman he'd ever been with.

"The locals drive chaotic. You have to watch out for them and their nimble fingers."

"I'll remember that." She gripped her bag tighter.

They walked along the beach, where she abruptly sat in the sand. She pulled a large pad and a couple of pencils from her bag.

"You're an artist." He sat crossed legged beside her, not touching.

"I am."

Her sketch slowly became clear. A tiny pink shell lying in the sand. Something he never noticed, yet she saw it immediately and drew it in perfect, minute detail. His gaze slid to her face. The breeze blew strands of her hair, and her head tilted as she added more detail of the sand around the tiny shell.

"I would have never seen it." He looked at the shell and back at her. "Beautiful."

She lifted her head and shiny lips spread into a smile. "I do that. Notice things most people don't. And yes, it is beautiful."

He chuckled. He couldn't help it. Any other woman would have assumed he was talking about them. This girl thought he was speaking of the seashell.

She leaned out, picked up the shell, and rubbed her thumb over the smooth surface. "Such a tiny thing, yet significant."

"*Benzinho.*"

"What?"

"Small."

She looked at the shell and repeated his word, mangling it with her accent. He stood and reached out his hand. "Come. We should get back to the boat."

She dropped her things into her bag, and looked up at him, hesitation in those expressive eyes, before she finally placed her hand in his.

THE NEXT MORNING, Angel ran the track with her headphones in, blaring Alien Ant Farm. The ship had everything, and this early there were very few people in the gym area. She hadn't been able to sleep. She'd spent most of the night trying to sort her feelings, or lack-there-of, for Thrand. It utterly confused her. She spent a good several years pining for him, and then a chunk of her savings on this trip she'd thought necessary to purge him. Yet all she felt was relief.

No pining.

No missing his face.

She was a fool.

Then she saw Cole. In loose shorts and a tank, he put weights on a barbell. The muscles in his arms flexed, and he was in his own zone, headphones stuck in his ears. She debated whether or not to stop, but her feet made the decision for her.

He looked up, his crooked smile appeared, and he pulled out an earbud. "Morning, Angel."

Goosebumps spread over her skin. His voice should be on lockdown. "Hi."

His caramel eyes zoomed over her sweaty form as he put more weight on the bar. "Early riser, too?"

"Yup. Jog every morning. Or yoga." Somewhere between last night and this morning she had lost the ability to carry on a conversation. Or maybe it was his damn voice at five a.m. Or his lips.

"What are you listening to?"

"Punk. What about you?"

"Somehow that doesn't surprise me. Latin."

They stood silent, staring at each other until it became utterly awkward. She turned to resume her run. "Have a good workout."

"Wait. Would you like to spend the day with me in San Juan?"

She paused. "Why?"

His brows shot up. "Why?"

"Yes, why. I'm sure there are plenty of other women you could enjoy your time with. I'm not your norm." *Bingo*. His flushed face said it all. "So I'm gonna let you off the hook, darlin'. Thanks for yesterday."

She shoved her bud back in her ear and took off, leaving him gaping. A shame, really. But the last thing she needed was to get tangled up with someone like that. Clean shaven and not a tattoo in sight, he wasn't her norm either. She highly doubted his wallet had a chain. After she made a complete lap, he stepped in front of her, forcing her to stop.

"You're right. You're not like any girl I've ever met. Maybe that's why I want to get to know you. Friends."

She put her hands on her hips. "Friends? That's all?"

He rubbed beneath his chin and nodded. "Yes."

"Lie." She crossed her arms over her chest.

He tugged her off the track, which had gotten busy enough that they were blocking traffic flow. "Not entirely."

His fingers touched hers lightly and whatever *that* was returned with a vengeance. The shock made her scalp prickle. His gaze lifted from their light touch to her face.

"You're different. Nice. Real. And…" He took a deep breath and glanced away. "I'd like to know someone *real*."

The way he emphasized the word real made

her heart jump in her throat. He slid his hands into his pockets and looked down. His uncertainty puzzled her. She was positive he was not a man used to being unsure of himself, or unsure of anything for that matter. This was not one of his cliché pick-up lines.

"Cole." He tilted his head to look at her. "Okay."

The slow smile that curved his lips sent her heart plummeting right to her feet. He touched her cheek. Just the barest hint of skin to skin.

"Thank you, *Anjinho Anjo.*"

"What does that mean?"

"Little angel. I will meet you on at the Pool Bar in a couple of hours, yes?"

She nodded. Her brain forced air into her lungs. He turned back to his weights and somehow she compelled her feet to move.

Little angel.

That's what he'd called her. She all but ran to her room and fell across her bed. She could still feel that tiny touch to her cheek. If nothing else, that should have warned her this was a mistake.

But what could really happen on a fourteen day cruise? It was just a blip of time in the whole scheme of things. She touched her face, stood, and looked in the mirror. Her pale skin was pink from more than just her run.

CHAPTER THREE

THE RAINFORESTS OF San Juan were breathtaking. Worth the all day tour Cole insisted they take. The waterfalls and the dense foliage was like nothing she had ever seen. The next day they were in Philipsburg. And another day spent with him.

Now they had a full day at sea, on their way to Half Moon Cay. Another place she'd never been. She sat on deck, under an umbrella, with her drawing pad in her lap, sketching out a waterfall she'd seen on San Juan.

Cole sat right beside her, a beer in his hand. "Can I see your drawings?"

Her first instinct was to refuse, but she turned toward him. Those warm eyes looked steadily back into hers and she handed him her pad.

"I never show anyone."

"Why not?" he asked as he flipped slowly through each page. She fiddled with her pencil as he paused on page after page of Thrand. "Is this a boyfriend?"

Of course he would ask. "No. That's Thrand, a regular in my dad's bar. I..." She hesitated and blew out a breath when Cole looked at her. "I had a stupid crush on him. He didn't return the feeling. Which is the entire reason I'm on this boat. To get some space, to figure out what I want to do with my life."

"Has it helped?" He continued to flip, pausing now and then to study one of her drawings.

"That's the funny part. I don't even miss him. I pined after the guy for years, and the first time I get away from him, I feel nothing at all. I'm a shallow fool."

A RUSH OF jealousy hit Cole as he looked at the many, many drawings of Thrand. But her words made him stop and focus on her. "You are neither shallow nor a fool. Those two things I am well acquainted with." Too acquainted with unfortunately.

"I wasted time waiting for him to notice me as more than a friend. I look back now, and all I did was wait. It's like I pushed a big pause button on my life." She huffed out a breath and shoved her hands in her hair. "I could have been doing something. Like pursuing my dreams."

"And what is your dreams?"

"Owning my own shop. Selling my art and the clothes I design."

Now the pin up style dresses drawn in her pad made sense. "So talented. This is your creation?"

He held up the pad to show one of the dresses. He knew nothing about clothes, but he had an eye for good design.

"Yup. A lot of the clothes I wear are mine. But all that talent is wasted sitting in my notepads."

He closed it and handed it back to her. "You may think you've wasted time, but now you have a stock full of art. When you go home, you can work on putting that dream into motion."

"I guess. And I have been saving money—until I blew a chunk on this cruise."

He rested his head against the deck chair and met her gaze. "Sometimes you have to get away to get perspective. I am here alone for a similar reason."

"Sorry, but I won't believe you're here because some girl didn't fall at your feet."

He chuckled when she rolled her eyes at him but the truth of his reality weighed like a stone. "No. But two years ago my wife died in a car crash. My life has been on hold ever since."

He didn't tell her the whole story. No one knew it in its entirety. Not even his family. He'd been numb these last two years, going through the motions. The cruise had been his last effort to snap out of it and get out from under his overbearing family. They meant well, but he just wanted some peace.

She reached out and held his hand, remorse in those deep blue eyes. "I am so sorry."

He took the opportunity to cling to her hand. He stared at her and tried to analyze just what she was making him feel. He knew what lust was. This was… more. Her face pinked, her lips parted, and he swung his feet so he faced her and sandwiched her hand between both of his. She attempted to pull her hand away, but he wouldn't let her.

"I believe things happen for a reason. Out of our control. Sometimes it has to be bad to get us where we are supposed to be." He turned her hand palm up and traced the faint creases.

Her eyes narrowed and her body stiffened. "What are you saying?"

"Not what you're thinking. And all that aside, this," he brushed his calloused thumb over her dainty hand, "is something. I don't know what it is, but it's there."

She jerked her hand away. "You said friends. That's all."

He leveled his eyes on her. "Are you telling me you don't feel it?"

He couldn't help but smile when she lifted her chin. "I think you're trying to play off my sympathies."

"You're the one who said I could have any girl I want. You're right, Angel. I haven't been with many but… I can. I have. Nothing was there."

"Then why the hell are you wasting your time with me? Go play with some Barbie and leave me alone." She swung her legs so their bare knees bumped.

Anger made her eyes spark and her small hands fisted. He placed his hands gently on either side of her face and leaned in closer. "Because you are different. Real. And whatever this flicker is, we both feel it. Are you not curious?"

"Lust," she spat. "Plain and simple."

He shook his head, and this thumb brushed along her lower lip. "No. Lust is—you see it. You want it. You take it. And you forget it. That is lust."

"Isn't that what you're attempting to do?"

"No. I want to get to know you. I like to see you smile and I want it to stay there. I want to know what makes you tick and what pushes you to the edge. I want to know what you think about. That has nothing to do with lust."

His breath came hard as he stared into her face. That perfect face with those expressive eyes. She couldn't hide her shock or the shadows of doubt that filled her mind.

"You're trying to play me." But her words lacked punch, and her bottom lip quivered.

"No. I'm not a player. Never have been."

"You just said you could have any girl you

want. That's the definition of a player."

"I can. Doesn't mean I do."

She sucked in a breath and jerked her head back so his hands fell away. "I don't know you or trust you. Just because I look like a stupid doll doesn't mean I am. I grew up around men who would make you piss yourself. So if you think you can get one over on me, you're in for a surprise."

"Wow. And I thought I had trust issues. I never thought you were a 'stupid doll' and I don't scare easily." He stood. "I don't know you, but I want to. I know there is more to you than what most people see. Too bad you're the one underestimating and judging me."

He left her sitting there, dodged families and honeymooners, and headed for his room. If she wanted to talk to him, she knew how to get a hold of him. He didn't know why he'd opened up as much as he had, but getting it tossed back in his face was not what he expected. The girl had walls. High, thick walls.

He'd never been jealous. It was odd and foreign. Never experienced it with Melanie, his deceased wife. It surprised him that he'd felt more with this little hell-cat than he ever had with her. Or anyone.

In his room, he sat down at his laptop. Work was what he should be doing. He needed to finish the layout of the house he was designing. He booted up his computer and stared out the large stretch of glass that led out to his balcony and the view of the endless ocean.

Would Angel contact him? What would he do if she didn't? Could he just let her go and always wonder what-if?

ANGEL STARED AT the empty lounge chair Cole had left. Her mind jumbled with all the things he'd said. She released a breath and fell back against the lounger. She'd felt it. She knew exactly what he was talking about, and no, she had never had that zing with anyone else. She instinctively fell back on her usual and shut him out. Except, he didn't act the way every other guy had.

He'd called her on it. Accused her of being the judgmental one.

She'd put on her bitch purposely and it worked.

He left.

She shoved her stuff in her bag, went straight to her room, and sat on her tiny balcony. Tears tracked down her face and she wiped at them angrily. Tears she thought she'd be shedding for Thrand, and yet he'd barely jarred her thoughts. Cole's warm brown eyes stayed in the forefront of her mind.

I like to see you smile and I want it to stay there. I want to know what makes you tick and what pushes you to the edge.

No one had ever said anything like that to her before. All the one-night-stands she'd had. Guys who declared their ever-lasting love and she hadn't felt a damn thing. She thought it was because she wanted Thrand.

She put her bare feet on the railing and put her chin in her hands.

No. What she wanted—was to be wanted. Someone to see her… *really see her.*

What if Cole was the only one to ever try?

Could she let her insecurities shut him out?

This entire trip so far had been one eye-opener after another and not in the way she'd anticipated.

SHE WATCHED THE sun sink into the water and sat alone. She'd looked at her phone a hundred times. Would he text?

He never did.

They were supposed to go ashore at Half Moon Cay tomorrow. It was almost the halfway mark of her trip. So she texted him.

You still talking to me?

C: *Of course. Just waiting for you.*

Waiting for me?

C: *To see if you would speak to me again.*

She paused. Any other guy would have been messaging her endlessly, wanting to know just what had crawled up her ass or begging for forgiveness. Then she would tell them who her family was and *poof,* they'd be gone. Having ties to a tough motorcycle gang did it every time.

She was about to text him again when there was a knock on her door. She got up and opened it.

"I thought this would be better than text. Come to dinner with me."

Cole stood in her doorway. A tingle spread over her skin before suspicion hit. "How did you know where my room was?"

He shoved his hands in his pockets and looked sheepish. "Would you believe a lucky guess?"

She raised a brow and placed a hand on her hip. She should be creeped out, but his dark skin blushed and he shifted on his feet. It was quite humorous to see him so uncomfortable.

"No?" He shook his head and sighed. "When you were looking for something in your bag and piled your stuff on the table, I noticed your room number on some papers."

She would give him that one 'cause she wasn't the most organized person. "So you thought you'd just show up at my door?"

"I don't like text." The sheepishness was gone, replaced by quiet intensity.

She licked her lips and nodded. "Let me change."

She left the door open as she turned, grabbed some clothes, and slipped into the bathroom while he stepped into the room and shut the door. She tugged on her snug Alien Ant Farm shirt and jean shorts. She ran a hand through her hair and then stepped into the room. They didn't match at all. He wore a white button down with rolled up sleeves and khaki shorts. The white only accentuated his dark skin and exotic looks.

And he looked good. Too good. Especially since he stood in front of her bed. It sent all sorts of wicked ideas spinning through her mind. His dark head lifted to stare at her and awareness prickled up her spine.

She hastily shoved her feet into her black Chucks. "Let's go."

Without waiting for him, she stepped into the hallway. That room was too small with him and all the tension between them. Except he was right behind her, his body close, his hand on the small of her back as he moved with her into the elevator. He leaned one shoulder on the wall, his head tilted down toward hers.

Don't look up. Don't look up.

She looked up and choked. He was so damn close. His eyes piercing hers. Her heart raced and she forced herself not to give in and shove up on her toes to taste those tempting lips. The door opened and he gave her a one sided smirk.

"After you."

He grabbed her hand and she didn't pull away. Instead, she curled her hand into his. She wanted him to know that she chose to leave it there. No matter her reservations or insecurities.

She met his surprised gaze head on while he led her to the restaurant.

CHAPTER FOUR

COLE LIKED HER straightforward honesty and the way she gripped his hand. He'd expected her to pull away. Instead, she tightened her grip and looked right at him. That told him everything he needed to know. Maybe, just maybe, she'd admitted to herself what he already knew.

A heady attraction that grew stronger by the minute.

They settled at a table near a wall of glass so they could look out over the water. It was almost dark, and light from the ship glinted off the ripples.

"So tell me about these men you grew up with." Cole took a bite of his salmon while she ate shrimp pasta. "The men who would scare me."

She tensed and folded her napkin. "I'm not sure you want to know."

"If I didn't, I wouldn't have asked."

She snorted. "A lot of people ask things when they don't really want the answer."

"Try me."

Silence hung as conflicting emotions flickered

across her face. She released a breath. "All right. But remember, you asked. You already know my dad runs Booseys, the bar I work at. My mom's brother runs Steel Grim. A motorcycle gang in Nashville. I grew up around them. They come into the bar quite often. Trust me when I say guys don't stick around long when they learn that tidbit of information."

He sat back and could tell by the look on her face she expected him to get up and leave. "This is supposed to scare me?"

"It should. They're not exactly nice and are very protective of their 'angel.'" The word 'angel' was said through clenched teeth and flashing eyes.

"I told you I don't scare easily."

"Yeah, well, you don't know them. They would eat you for lunch." She threw her napkin. "This is pointless."

She shoved back her chair and shot to her feet. He grabbed her hand and tugged her back down.

"You are underestimating me again." His brows lowered over his eyes.

"You don't get it—"

He stood abruptly, cutting her off, and with her hand still in his, took off out the door to the deck, dragging her with him. His emotions rode high and he never lost his cool.

He was tired of her assumptions.

Tired of her judgments.

Tired of fighting his attraction to her.

He strode purposely to an empty area.

"Cole, really, this is—"

"This is what you don't get." Cole spun her, pressed her back against the ship and claimed her mouth.

His hands gripped each side of her head as he caught her gasp. Her small hands tightened in his shirt as he swept his tongue along the seam of her lips. How he wanted to dive in deep, but instead, molded his body to hers. Her lithe curves fit nicely into the hard planes of his form. He dropped his head and placed a lingering kiss just behind her ear. Blood raced hotly through his veins when she arched closer.

She stirred him up in ways he didn't understand. She'd labeled him. As what, he didn't know, but he wanted to redefine her classification of him. He wasn't a boy. He knew who he was and what he wanted. At the moment, it was the irresistible and infuriating woman in his arms.

His thumbs traced the delicate bones of her face as her breath came out in small puffs. He fell into her dark gaze.

"I'm not like others. Do *not* compare me to them," he whispered.

ANGEL WAS STUNNED. He'd been so polite and passive… she never saw this coming. Her body reacted instantly. His scent, the faint taste of Corona on those lips that lured her. But he kept them from her, denying her the pleasure. A mere taste wasn't enough.

She wanted more. Wanted him.

Had from the moment he'd spoken with that enticing accent. That hard body against hers only confirmed it, and she was done ignoring what he'd been trying to tell her. What she already knew.

Who the hell cared who her family was? She was on a cruise, a thousand miles away from her real world. This would only be a fling anyway, right? She jerked her mind out of the rut where she'd been spinning her wheels and focused on the here and now. She wanted him, and there was no one to tell her she couldn't have him.

She rose up on her toes and slid an arm around his neck.

"Just kiss me."

His mouth hovered over hers. So close, yet so far away. She tried to reach for him, but he held back. The anticipation only ramped up her want. She pulled him so his lips landed on hers.

That shot right through her. She clung to him. No longer holding back, the force of his kiss overtook her and left no doubt who was in charge. His tongue sparred with hers, his teeth tugged at her lower lip, he angled her head so all she could do was open for him. Her legs shook and her body burned from the inside out. She hooked a leg around his hip, wanting him closer. Strong hands dug hard into her ass. He ground into the *v* of her legs and her head fell back, her lungs searching for air. His hard bulge teasing her.

He stopped, his breath hot and heavy on her neck. "You want this?"

She was barely able to breathe, much less talk, so she lowered her hands and shoved them under the hem of his shirt. The smooth, taunt skin of his abs contracted under her fingertips.

"*Querida*? My room?" Every time he said something in Portuguese or Spanish it made her body tingle and something warm settled low. She rarely knew what he said but it didn't matter. His voice was like smooth bourbon. He could cuss her, and it would still turn her on.

She nodded, worked her hands partway up his back. She tipped her head so she could see his face in the dim light. His eyes were closed and a muscle ticked in his jaw.

"You test my patience." He kissed her hard, and everything faded before he abruptly pulled back. She stumbled when he grabbed her hand to lead her to a set of elevators.

People were inside, but Cole didn't seem to care. He pulled her so her back was to his chest.

With his arm tight around her waist, he dropped his head so his mouth was against her ear.

"I want to hear you scream my name, *Anjinho Anjo*," he whispered.

Her knees threatened to buckle. He'd called her *Little Angel* again. She hated her name, but not when he said it.

She barely recognized the fact that most people had gotten off, yet they were still going up. The doors opened on the Seventeenth Deck and he led her out.

"Uh, Cole."

"Yes?" he asked as he led her through a fancy foyer to room number 1758. He swiped his card and the door popped open.

"Holy shit," she muttered under her breath as he pulled her inside and shut the door. "You're rich."

"Does it matter?" He crowded her against the door.

He blocked her view of the spacious room and his hands skated along her arms, then pinned them above her head. She tugged, but they were firmly anchored.

She gulped in air. "You never said anything."

"I ask you again, does it matter?"

How had she ever thought this man passive? He unbuttoned her shorts and with space between them, she should have been able to think. She had agreed to come here but with a calloused thumb tracing the line of her panties, she couldn't even remember what he asked.

"Yes, I have money, but I don't go around announcing it. This is your last chance if you want to go." His thumb dipped just under the hem and stopped.

Her body thrummed with the need he'd ignited. Her hips arched automatically, wanting more. She licked her lips. "I don't care, just move, dammit."

He kicked her feet a little wider and shoved a long finger inside her. Her head banged on the door as every nerve ending sparked to life. "Yes," she hissed.

She bucked against his hand, not caring that the only part of him touching her was his hand on her wrists and his other hand fucking her senseless with not one but two fingers.

"I have to taste you," he ground out.

He shoved at her shorts and panties, leaving them at a pile at her feet. He knelt, yanked off her shoes, hooked one leg over his shoulder, and replaced his deft fingers with his mouth.

She gripped his hair and screamed his name. All thought wiped out. His hands gripped her ass as she struggled not to fall. Hot pleasure surged through her as wave after wave hit.

"Need," she panted and pulled at his shirt.

He took his time getting to his feet. His mouth, lips, and teeth tasting and teasing his way up as he shoved her shirt over her head, taking her bra with it, and dropped it. His mouth claimed a hard nipple, and she curled her naked body around his fully dressed one. He picked her up, and she locked her legs around his waist. His teeth pulled and teased her breast sending tiny little shocks of pain and pleasure through her body.

"You have way too many clothes on," she muttered as she shoved a hand down the back of his shirt. He walked further into the room, dropped her to the couch, yanked off his shirt, and kicked off the rest of his clothes.

Cole naked was breathtaking. She'd seen him without a shirt, but all of him was that same dusky colored skin. She circled a hand around his cock and he groaned.

"Not this time." He dropped to his knees again and she surged forward with impatience. His muscles jumped under her touch as she explored his chest and shoulders, and her mouth found his again. Her taste in his mouth only spurred her on. She wanted him in her. Now.

He fumbled with his shorts until she heard the crackle of foil. She raked her nails up his neck. He pulled her hips to the edge of the couch and slammed in.

Breath left her. He filled her, stretched her,

and when he moved, stars appeared behind her eyes. "Oh hell," she whimpered.

She clenched the back of the couch as he pounded hard, fast. The gentleman was gone. His hands cupped her ass so her legs draped carelessly over both arms. His gaze skimmed her body, but she couldn't keep her eyes open. Her head fell back, her body nothing but sensation. He slowed and she panted. His big, rough, hands slid up her back making her arch like a cat.

"*Gostosa*," he murmured against her mouth.

A shudder rippled through her as he pulled out. He whipped her around so her knees hit the floor, her elbows buried into the cushions. He slid in again and her body jerked and spasmed around him.

His hands skated along her curves, cupped a breast, then tweaked a nipple. She cried out. A total out of body experience. But he didn't move. He held her tight, firmly buried in her. He spread his knees, which spread hers.

"Beautiful." He kissed along her neck and his thumb pressed against her clit.

"Move. Please move," she begged.

"Tell me what you want, *Anjo*. Do you wish me to rub this?" His thumb moved a fraction.

"Yes," she panted.

"How about this?" He cupped a breast and tweaked a nipple.

She nodded, breath wasn't necessary, but his hands on her were. "Anything. Please."

All it took was a few quick moves. "Cole," she cried out as her nails dug into the couch.

Then he drove in hard, completing her. Filling her as he pulsed deep within.

ANGEL WOKE, CONFUSED and dazed, with a warm body pressed against her back. Every muscle ached. She turned slowly and looked up into Cole's sleeping face. They'd had sex. She'd lost count of how many times.

She sucked in her lower lip and scooted out from under his arm. Panic descended. She had to get out of here. She stopped when she spotted a fireplace in his bedroom.

They were on a cruise ship and the guy had a fucking fireplace in a *separate* bedroom. She looked around for her clothes. Nothing. He'd stripped her at his door. She snuck a glance at his sleeping form. The blankets were a tangled mess low on his waist. His dark brown hair was mussed and sexy as sin. And those lips… what he could do with those lips. She bit back a groan and pulled her gaze away. If she stared at him much longer, she would crawl back in with him.

She crept out of his room and blinked. He'd had her too occupied to notice anything last night. There was a kitchenette, an office area, a couch and love seat, and a piano… a baby grand piano.

Holy hell. This guy was loaded.

She shook her head, hurried to her clothes, yanked them on, and stepped out of the room. Thankfully, the elevator was right there. She hurried inside and pushed button six. Huddled into a corner, she didn't meet anyone's gaze as they came and went. Finally in her room, she hopped into her shower, turned it on as hot as it would go and stayed until the water turned cold.

She still felt his hands.

His mouth.

His body.

Everywhere.

She didn't wanted to erase it, but her entire being had shifted on its axis. She wasn't a prude. She'd been with guys of all types. From the geeky to the tough motorcycle dude loaded with tattoos. None long term, of course. Hard to do that when you had a family like hers.

But none of them made her feel what Cole did.

That had turned into a raging inferno.

Lust, plain and simple.

No matter what Cole had tried to tell her before, as far as she could see, he did exactly what lust did. He saw, he wanted, and he took.

And oh hell, did he take.

Last night he owned every tiny molecule of her. Cole hid a very dominant side. No denying she'd relished every moment of it.

She'd just dried her hair when there was a knock on her door. She closed her eyes. She could pretend she wasn't there and didn't know who was really at the door, but she'd be lying to herself if she thought she didn't want to see him again.

So she took a deep breath and opened the door. Cole's eyes pierced her. Stripped her with one look. She swallowed and backed up. He walked in and shut the door.

"Why did you leave without a word?"

His hair was damp and she fisted her hands to keep them out of those silky strands. "I wanted to shower."

He cocked a brow. "Which would explain leaving without a word."

She braved a tremulous smile while she quivered on the inside. "We were done. I didn't think it mattered—"

"It mattered to me." He advanced on her and gently held one of her hands. His thumb—*that thumb*—brushed along the pulse inside her wrist. "I wanted to have breakfast with you. Talk to you."

"Well, you're in luck. I haven't eaten. And you are talking to me. So, I say it's a win."

He frowned, released her, and shoved a hand through his wet hair. He took a step back and, heaven save her, but that was the last thing she wanted. Her body hummed and vibrated with all the wicked things he'd done to her last night.

She craved it.

Craved him.

Again.

She clenched her hands behind her back.

"I wanted to wake up with you."

His voice was low and it buzzed right through her. She never spent the night with anyone she slept with. He'd been the first. "Why?" Was she asking him or herself?

He leaned casually against the tiny desk in the room and a smile flickered briefly before it was gone. "Come here."

Those words alone made her legs shake. She shouldn't; she tried to fight it, but in the end, she stepped toward him. He snaked an arm around her waist and pulled her between his legs. "Because of this."

He lips barely touched hers. His fingertips skimmed her cheek.

She waited with bated breath, and her heart beat out of her chest. Surely he would kiss her harder?

"You missed your good morning kiss."

CHAPTER FIVE

COLE STARED AT Angel. She wanted. He could see it in her eyes. In the way her tongue slid across her lips, and the pulse that beat staccato at her neck. Why did she run? She had to have known he would come for her.

"I don't do good morning kisses," she breathed.

"Why not?"

"Cause I don't spend the night, so there is no good morning."

"Is that why you left?"

"We were done."

"Are we?"

He dropped his hands and braced them on the desk behind him. He wasn't holding onto her or touching her. Would she step away from him?

For a brief moment, panic filled her stormy gaze. She moved away and disappointment swept through him.

"You had your fun. Time to move on to your next conquest."

His range of emotions was short. Never extreme either way, but this girl pushed him. "Didn't we already go through this? I am not a player."

"Really?" She crossed her arms. "I've been in your room. You're rich as fuck. You lied."

He glared at her. "You think because someone has money it means they're a player? And I never lied to you."

"You said you built houses. Last I checked no one makes that kind of money building houses."

"Are you listening to yourself? I own CR Designs. I design and build custom homes." He laced his hands in front of him to keep his rising anger in check. "You are infuriating, you know that? My salary has nothing to do with what happened between us."

"We had sex, Cole. That's all."

That did it. In one swift move, he was on her and they tumbled onto her small couch. He lay half on top of her, one knee braced on the floor, the other between her legs. His hands tangled in her cropped hair, and his mouth slammed on hers. She moaned into his kiss, her hands already under his shirt. He pulled back abruptly. Her glazed eyes looked up at him.

"Just sex?"

Her pert mouth parted but no words escaped.

"I want to have breakfast with you and take you to explore Half-Moon Cay. Will you come with me?"

Still she said nothing.

"I'll take that as yes."

COLE SET UP the umbrella canopy and looked at Angel, who stood at the water's edge in her little red bikini. Waves lapped around her ankles. Her pale skin held a hint of color from the sun, but was nowhere near tan status. The blue of the water was a beautiful backdrop for her petite frame. She was a complicated contradiction. He could have taken her right there in her room not moments after she called him a liar.

The memory of her taste lingered. That awareness he'd sensed the first time he'd touched her was now a full-blown need. He wasn't a player. Had only been with a handful of women since Melanie died. And he certainly didn't feel the need to dominate them.

Only Angel brought that out in him. No longer numb, he wanted to stroke her skin, watch her face while she called out his name… totally out of character for him. Beyond that, he wanted more than just her body. And he had seven more days to prove to her she wasn't just another girl.

Her lips pressed into a thin line. She was thinking too much, and he wanted that smile. The one that made him smile back.

He ran toward her, scooped her up, and tossed her over his shoulder while she squealed with laughter. They fell into the water, dunking them both. They came up spewing water. He grinned when she splashed him.

"What was that for?" she asked and pushed her wet hair from her face before balancing her hands on his shoulders.

Water droplets clung to her lashes and those unbelievable storm blue eyes stared up at him. With an arm around her waist, her body was flush against his. That spark flared to life.

"I wanted to see your smile." His words came out in a hush as his heart picked up a beat.

Her smile changed to parted lips.

He brushed a knuckle along her jaw. He lowered his head, and her breath rushed out over his lips. He hovered. Waited. Met her gaze and wanted her to feel what he did. Her fingers curled tight on his shoulders.

He dropped his lips to hers. She tasted salty from the sea as he nibbled and kissed her. Nothing existed except the rush that swept through him and the girl in his arms.

Just like in her room, she came alive. Her hands slid over his shoulders and into his hair. She locked her legs around his waist and wiggled her hips so she rode along his erection. Her heels dung into his back, and with nothing between them but thin scraps of wet fabric, he wanted a taste of her passion.

"You test my control," he said into her ear.

Her answer was a pant and a nip at his neck. He seized her hips and rocked her hard against him. Luckily, they were at the very end of the cay where he had rented a cabana, and there were very few people this far out. They were in deep enough water no one would know for sure what they were doing.

He scraped his teeth just under her ear and she bucked hard. "I want you to come like this. Teasing me while you get yourself off."

Her half-lidded gaze met his as he helped her move. Her eyes closed while the water churned around them. She trembled, and he captured her kitten mewls with his mouth. She left new marks on his back as she hit her high.

Her head fell on his shoulder as he held her. When her body finally relaxed, she lifted her head, and he couldn't help but grin. A blush spread across her cheeks.

"Are you embarrassed?"

Her cheeks reddened even more and she buried her face in his neck. "No."

He laughed. "You are."

He took a few deep breaths to lesson his libido. He didn't want to humiliate himself by walking to shore with a raging hard on. He started to carry her back, but she shot out of his arms, swam until she could reach the bottom, and walked to shore.

His attention strayed to the way her ass swayed side to side. They both dried off in silence and he found it amusing that she wouldn't meet his gaze.

"I'm going to get us a drink, I'll be back."

She nodded but still wouldn't look at him as she plopped down under the canopy and shoved on her sunglasses. He smirked and strode to the nearest bar, a ways down the beach. She needed some space and so did he.

The chemistry between them jarred him. Nothing compared. Not even his wife. He'd met Melanie when he was fifteen. She was the daughter of his parents' business partners, and even though they'd waited until after college to get married, everyone had always assumed they would. Did they get married because it was expected? Because they were comfortable with each other? She had been a safe bet. At least he used to think so.

He remembered so vividly the last time he saw her alive. She'd gotten into her car, and had to push the seat back to accommodate her ever-growing middle. The roads were getting bad and they had been arguing. He told her to stay home.

She hadn't listened.

A lump lodged in his throat. It'd been two years. Guilt ate at him. He should have forced her to stay home.

He shook his head when the guy behind the counter yelled at him. "You ordering or what?"

He asked for a beer and a sex-on-the-beach for Angel and took his time heading back to their spot.

Half Moon Cay was probably the most beautiful stop on the entire cruise. Luckily they would be docking here again before the end of the two weeks. He paused when Angel came into view.

He grappled with how she was forcing him to feel something other than guilt and remorse. She made him feel extremes. Nothing subtle about it. About her. He moved in closer and sat beside her under the shade.

"Your favorite drink." He handed her a glass.

Her sunglasses were off and she was drawing in her sketchpad again. She met his gaze, took the glass, and then a sip. "Thanks."

"What are you drawing this time?"

She paused then showed him. It was a tall man walking away down a beach. He jerked his gaze up to meet hers.

"Yes. That's you." Her knees were curled to her chest, her head braced on her hand, mystery in her eyes.

He looked at the drawing again. It was done in pencil, but she had outlined every muscle in his back. The shading hinting to a darker skin tone.

"That's how you see me?"

"What do you mean?"

"I look confident." He didn't feel it. Not

since… then.

A smile flitted across her face and his heart skipped a beat. "You are."

"You should always smile." He touched the corner of her lips. "And I'm not. I'm a little surprised you see me that way."

Her eyes widened. "Are you kidding? You are one of the most confident people I've ever met."

"Even after our first meeting?"

She laughed. "Yes. Even after you sorta made a fool of yourself. But a cute fool."

He reached over and pulled her sideways into his lap. She squeaked but didn't protest. He couldn't help himself. He didn't think he'd been called cute since he was a kid. "How does everything you do make me want to touch you?"

He cupped the back of her neck and stared into her face, memorizing every curve, and the way her dark eyes lightened when she laughed.

"How come every time you touch me I can't breathe?" she asked in a whisper.

He tightened his hold on her while his pulse ricocheted through his body. "Make a deal with me."

Her arm draped lazily around his neck, but her fingers dug into his skin. "What?"

"From here on out, let's drop the walls. Nothing but honesty and truth between us."

She stiffened. "Why? In eight days this will be

over."

"Does it have to be?"

"You're talking crazy." She tried to get off his lap but he tightened his hold.

"Maybe. But what do we have to lose?"

ANGEL'S HEART THUNDERED in her chest. She really had no idea what he was asking of her. Drop her walls? She wasn't so dense that she didn't know she had walls, but damn, he always called her out on her shit. It was bad enough he'd gotten her off in the water. Totally not what she'd planned, but she hadn't lied. She forgot how to breathe when he touched her.

Right now, with his hands tracing her jaw and neck, thinking was a chore.

"You can't be serious? We've only known each other six days."

"So what? If I'm willing to chance it, why not you?"

"What exactly are we chancing?" She choked on the words as his lips inched closer. His eyes were warm caramel. Just like her favorite candy.

"I'm not even sure, so I will start with a truth. No one has made me feel what you make me feel. I'm even-tempered. I never feel strongly about anything."

"Lie."

"With you it's not." The corner of his mouth quirked up.

She gaped and her stomach dropped. Shit. "Are you always this open with strangers?"

He laughed. "*Anjinho Anjo,* we are not strangers."

As if his voice wasn't bad enough, he leaned in and kissed her lightly. She hated his light kisses. They made her want more. Made her want him to kiss her senseless. Made her want to crawl all over him. It took all her self-control not to bite his lip.

"All right. I'll give you that one."

"Why are you fighting this?"

"Cause this is ridiculous. Crazy. Nuts. Makes no sense. I shouldn't feel anything for you. I should be crying in my beer over Thrand. I should not be sitting in your lap wishing I was riding you instead. I should be able to breathe just fine when you're around. I don't understand, and it scares the hell out of me." Her chest heaved as she tried to scramble and save herself from everything she'd just dumped on him.

"Finally," he muttered before his mouth landed hard on hers.

She clenched his hair as he drowned every bit of thought and drenched her with nothing but feeling. A buzz started at her toes and sizzled right up her spine. She almost hit him when he broke the kiss.

"You tell me this is not worth giving a chance. You give me a real reason."

She gulped in air. She had nothing. "Truth?"

He pressed his forehead to hers. "Truth."

"Fear."

"Me too."

Fuck… That was not what she wanted to hear.

CHAPTER SIX

ANGEL STARED AT herself in the mirror. She wore a black, high-waist pencil skirt that stopped just above her knees, paired with a white and black striped off the shoulder shirt. She finished it off with red heels.

When she tried to apply matching red lipstick, her hand shook. She capped it, slapped it on the counter, and closed her eyes.

Cole had asked her to dinner tonight at Nu Soul Jazz. They'd spent almost the entire time together since she boarded. Eating with him should be no big deal.

Except… it was a big deal. She pressed her hand to her stomach as it did flip-flops. She couldn't remember the last time she'd been on a real date. And yeah, they already had sex, but he was asking for a solid shot. Walls down. Bare-it-all and see what happens.

She looked back into the mirror.

What if he really saw her?

With a deep breath, she grabbed her clutch and went to meet him. People stared. She ignored them. This was her style, and she'd learned to not care what others thought.

On the Deck Four, she walked inside the dimly lit bistro. Jazz music played low from the small stage at the back. She loved the moodiness of the sound. Glancing around, she didn't see him, so stepped up to bar, and was immediately waited on. She tapped her black nail impatiently.

A guy sat on a stool beside her and looked her up and down like she was for sale. "I'm so glad you made it. I've been waiting for you all my life."

She arched a brow. Working in a bar, she'd heard every line. Including that one. The guy was older, had a touch of gray at his temples and a faint line where his wedding band should be.

"Sorry. I'm expecting someone."

"Yeah. Me." His words were slurred and lines etched his brow.

"Divorced recently?"

He paled, took a swig of his beer then shoved a hand through his hair. "Am I that transparent? How heartwarming."

"Happens to the best."

COLE WALKED INTO the Jazz club and stopped. Angel wore an outfit that clung to her every curve. He loved her unique style, and his fingers itched to touch her. He stepped up behind her, placed a hand at her waist. She laid her small one over his and looked up. No surprise on her face. A thrill shot through him because she'd known who he was without looking.

"I have a table reserved for us in the back." He glanced at the gentleman she was talking to. "You don't mind, do you?"

"Not at all. It was a pleasure talking to your lady." He tossed down some bills and nodded to Angel. "Thanks for humoring me for a little while. Enjoy your evening." With that he walked out.

Angel remained silent, but she gripped Cole's hand while they were led to a booth.

"You look beautiful."

She smiled faintly. "Thanks."

They made small talk while they ate. Once the plates were cleared, he stared at her intently.

"Why are you nervous?" he asked.

"Because this feels like a real date," she said, and lifted her eyes to his.

"It is. But why does that make you nervous?"

"This 'truth' thing is harder than I thought," she muttered under her breath and took a drink of her wine. "I've never really dated much. Not in a traditional sense. I can't remember the last time I've been on one."

The curved booth was private, the music low and set a mood. Which was what he was going for.

He wanted to be able to talk. Carry on a conversation without blaring sounds and flashing lights. He stretched his arm out behind her and turned so he faced her.

"I haven't dated much either since my wife died."

She laid a hand over his. Concern marked her brow and he could tell she wanted to ask but didn't.

"I'd known Melanie since I was a teenager. She was the daughter of my dad's business partner. It was assumed we would get married because we got along well. I'm not sure now that was a wise decision. The last year before she died, things had been difficult. There were... issues." He looked away, knowing he wasn't telling her the whole story. Some things he couldn't share yet.

"Since I work in a bar, I hear all these sob stories and I've learned what to say, but I got nothing except I'm sorry for your loss. There isn't a time frame on mourning the loss of someone you love." She lowered her chin and a slight frown marred her face.

"You've lost someone?"

"My mom had some complications while she was pregnant with my baby brother. I was six. We lost him." She turned her hand up and laced her fingers with his. "I don't think she ever got over it."

He swallowed and stared at their entwined hands. Should he tell her? He opened his mouth but he couldn't get the words out. It was too soon.

"I look at my cousin, Ethan, and wonder if he would've been like him. Tall and dark," she said.

He forced himself to look at her. Sadness lingered in her eyes. "Is this another guy I should be scared of?"

"Ethan? Probably. But he hasn't been in my life long. He's about six-five and big. Lots of tats. He's the lead singer of DirtSlap, a band he started with Thrand." She paused briefly. "As soon as I get back to Nashville, he's headed off to Vegas to get married."

Ethan or Thrand was getting married, but that's not what caught his attention. "You say 'married' like it's a bad word."

"Isn't it? He hadn't known this girl six months before he proposed to her... on stage no less. I know I'm not going to the wedding." She tapped her finger on the rim of her drink.

He arched a brow and watched her eyes flash. She always seemed cool and composed. He preferred the spark, but at the moment it wasn't clear what was causing it. "Why not?"

"Mom and Dad are going, so I offered to stay and watch the bar. Honestly, I would have made up any excuse not to go. Not really into that mushy shit."

"You don't like soft music and candles? Or don't like the idea of Thrand getting married."

"What? No, Ethan's getting married, not Thrand. Not that I really care." She snorted and gave him a look. "And no. Soft music and candles are out."

He pulled her closer, one hand on her hip, the other around the back of her neck. His thumb tipped her head up so he could look into her eyes. They dilated and her breath stalled.

"I'll keep that in mind."

"You do that."

"So what is it you do like?"

She licked her lips and her hand fisted his shirt. "You already know."

"Do I?"

She pressed her lips near his ear. "Truth. I like your control. And I like it more when your control breaks."

"Truth. I've never lost control before, but I don't have any where you're concerned." He squeezed her hip and her sexy laugh made him grit his teeth.

"Nice to know," she purred against his skin.

He angled his head so his lips skimmed her cheek. "And right now you're about to snap my control."

COLE WOKE WITH a start and jerked up. Relief

swept through him when he saw her beside him. She slept on her stomach, her arms curled beneath her, and her face turned away from him. He propped himself up on an elbow and tugged down the blankets. Perfect, pale skin spread out before him. The large tattoo on her shoulder stared up at him. It was a cross between a pin up and a day-of-the-dead girl's face. Done in gray, purple, and green, her purple eyes with the long lashes seemed to bore into him. What he found most interesting was a hole in her forehead in the shape of a heart with a green butterfly fluttering out. Knowing Angel, it meant something.

He pushed up her cropped hair and placed a kiss at the base of neck. She sighed, but didn't move. He resisted the urge to press up against her. They'd gotten very little sleep last night. He was insatiable where she was concerned. The more he tasted, the more he wanted. He slid out of bed, took a quick shower, pulled on loose shorts and went to start some coffee. He poured a cup and walked out onto his spacious balcony. They were docked in Ft. Lauderdale today, but this side of the ship didn't face the shore. All he saw was an endless stretch of blue.

The reasons he shouldn't let her in were long and numerous. But he was tired of hiding. Tired of running from the truth. The big fat ugly truth that he hadn't revealed to Angel last night. He hadn't lied, but he'd held back that last bit of info. He'd kept the secret for over two years—it wasn't an easy thing to let go of.

About an hour later, he heard her get up, so he called room service then went back on the deck and faced the open glass sliding door into his room. Would she take off again?

She walked into his view and his breath caught. She wore the black shirt he had worn under his button down the previous night. It hung loose on her and grazed her knees. She paused directly in his line of sight before she spotted him and walked his way.

Air rushed out of his lungs in relief. She was staying.

Her eyes widened when she glanced around his balcony. "Holy shit. You could have a party out here. There's even a hot tub."

"I'm not much into parties."

Her gaze swung back to him, and he stepped forward to tilt her face up. It was free from any trace of makeup, and he was taken in.

A quizzical look came over her face. "What?"

"You don't have any makeup on." Entranced, he traced her cheek.

"Uh, is that bad?" She tried to back up, but he snaked an arm around her waist.

"I've never seen a woman without makeup. Ever."

ANGEL DROWNED IN his eyes. In the way he looked at her. Like she was the most important thing he'd ever seen. Her stomach flipped. Her palms were damp and she didn't really understand his reaction. It didn't help that he was sexy as sin in nothing but those loose shorts. His chiseled body was a feast for the eyes.

"Not even your mom? Or your wife?"

He shook his head and pulled her between his legs as he leaned his back against the railing. "Nor my sisters. All the women in my life pride themselves on their looks. That means a perfect face."

She narrowed her gaze not sure if he was complimenting her or not. "What am I missing here?"

"You're real. So real." His thumbs grazed along her cheeks, across her lips. "You look so young. Please tell me you're legal."

She rolled her eyes. She knew she looked young, especially with no make-up on. "Yes. I'm twenty-five, but—"

"I'm thirty-two," he mumbled absently. "I'm not sure I would care how old you were at this point."

His teeth scraped along her lower lip then his hands cupped her ass and picked her up, forcing her to lock her legs around his waist. He carried her through the doors, placed her on the countertop, and stepped closer between her legs.

Thought came to a screeching halt as he angled her hips, tangled his other hand in her hair, and tugged her head back. His lips skimmed along her neck. Pinned, all she could do was grip his arms while he took his sweet time. Slow and deliberate. Her body wasn't hers anymore, yet she dug her heels into his ass, wanting him closer.

"You are the most real person I've ever met in my life." His words were nothing but air over her skin. "And I'm not sure I'll ever get enough of you."

He bit at her neck, and her hands shot into his hair. Her heart pounded out of her chest. His words and body took her piece-by-piece. By the time this cruise was over, would there be any part of her he hadn't taken?

A knock at the door had him growling against her skin. He lifted his head, his eyes glazed with passion and something deeper. Something that made her insides freeze.

"That would be our breakfast." He brushed his lips against her ear. "Don't move."

She sucked in her lip as he walked toward the door. His back was perfect except for the long red scratches on his skin from her nails. She couldn't stop the heat that hit her face as a tray was rolled in.

The man in uniform stalled as he stared at her,

which only made her blush worse. She couldn't imagine what she looked like, perched on the counter with nothing but Cole's shirt on.

Cole cleared his throat. "I understand the lure, but eyes on me, man."

The guy's face turned beet red and he mumbled an apology. Cole tipped him before he left.

The intense look he'd been giving her was gone, or at the very least, hidden, but she couldn't get it out of her head. Soon he was right back where he'd been before the interruption. Standing between her legs. She shoved a shaky hand through her hair.

He grabbed it and laced his with hers. "What is it?"

She shook her head. She couldn't name it because she didn't even know. His fingers grazed her face and tipped her chin up.

"Nothing," she said finally.

"Lie."

She tried to slide off the counter, but he trapped her with his body.

"We said no walls. So what is it?"

She took a deep breath, sat up straight and looked him in the eye. "Everything is progressing so fast. I don't do dates, I don't do relationships, and now it feels like I'm doing both. You tell me what this is. I don't even know you—"

"Stop. I know you think because it's only been

a few days you don't know me, but you do. You know me better than some who have known me my whole life." He stepped back and tugged at her hand. "Come here, I want to show you something."

CHAPTER SEVEN

CURIOUS TO WHAT he was up to, she let him lead her to an L-shaped desk where he turned on his laptop. He sat and pulled her into his lap. When the screen came on, she saw one of the most beautiful homes she'd ever seen. It was huge, with a circle drive, and tall pines surrounding it. It looked like an oversized and elegant log cabin. She looked over at him and noticed he watched her not the screen.

"That's my home. I designed and built it." He turned his attention to the screen and pushed a button to show another view. "There's a pond behind it."

"You love it." She could tell by the tone of his voice his home meant a lot to him.

He nodded. "I do. But mostly, I love the workshop I built out behind it." Another picture of a smaller version of the big house. "I build furniture as a hobby and this is where I spend every moment I can."

He flicked through photo after photo of his workshop, which was really a mini-house, complete with kitchen and living room. But what amazed her was the handcrafted furniture he built. Ornate hutches, handmade toys, and even a door with an elaborate carving in the middle, all done by him.

She picked up his hand. "It's why you have callouses."

"Yes. I also help build some of the houses I design. This is the house I'm currently working on." He clicked on a floor plan and pointed out what each room was. Before long, she understood the drawing.

"It's huge."

"About twelve thousand square feet."

Her jaw dropped and she turned to him. "That's insane. Who would need a home that big unless you had fifteen people living with you?"

He smiled and kissed the side of her neck. "I'm not sure. My home is nine thousand and it was just two people."

She blinked at him. "That doesn't even make sense. I live in an eight hundred square foot loft where everything is in one room except the bathroom. And it's plenty."

He cupped the back of her neck and spoke softly into her ear. "Yet another thing that makes you so real."

He started clicking through pictures of his family. Naming each one and talking about them.

"This is Casey, the oldest. She is thirty-eight and has three kids. Mitchell is thirty-four. He's the player of the family. Luke is twenty-eight and has four kids. And finally, the troublemakers. Adam and Amelia, the twins, are twenty-three. My parents are Leo and Josetta."

His low voice tickled her ear, drawing her into his world. Almost everyone was smiling or laughing, and it was clear where Cole had gotten his exotic looks. His mother was beautiful, with thick dark hair and the eyes that Cole had inherited. His father was a big man with blond hair and striking green eyes. Half his siblings looked like their mother, and the other half took after their dad.

"Do all of them live in Denver?"

"No. Just the twins and I. The rest are scattered all over the globe. But family is extremely important to my mother and they love to travel. We always pick a place to meet for holidays."

He continued to click through photos. So many of all of them together. For Christmas, Thanksgiving, birthdays, vacations. Cole pointed out and named everyone except for one tall blond woman. That had to be his deceased wife.

"My father was in Brazil on business when he met my mother. She loves to tell the story of their whirlwind courtship. Her family used to hate my dad because he took her away from them, but they have long gotten over it. Or at least tolerate it. Dad bought a home there so they can go back whenever they want."

At some point, he moved the food to his desk, and they ate while they relaxed and he talked. His hand brushed back and forth on her neck. The love for his family was evident with each story he told.

"You don't play fair, you know," she said as she absorbed his intent.

"I don't want you to ever say you don't know me. Ever again."

He stared into her face, and her body shivered. Her heart expanded and she took a deep breath. There was so much going on behind his eyes. A question hung there but he wouldn't ask.

He cupped her face. "No walls, *Anjo*."

She managed a nod. Seven more days of Cole and his caramel eyes.

THE NEXT SEVERAL days flew by in a blur. They visited each isle, Half Moon Cay, again, Ocho Rios, and Georgetown. They hit all the shops on the boat. They did the zip line and attended the theater. He didn't let her dwell on anything, kept her laughing, and owned her body every night. She told him about her family and showed him pictures on her phone.

They didn't talk about the future, only focusing on the here and now. But the more wrapped up she got in him, the louder the clock ticked. Every day the noose tightened around her neck. What happened when the cruise was over?

Day twelve was spent at sea. She was almost frantic, but hoped she managed to hide it. She didn't want to be the first to bring it up. She'd gotten so used to sleeping next to his large, warm frame, she didn't know how she'd ever sleep alone again. Or more to the point, she didn't know how she would sleep without him.

She sat on the couch, drawing in her notepad, and he was at the desk, working on his latest floor plan and answering emails for his business. Except she couldn't concentrate, her gaze kept straying back to him. Those large hands, those too full lips, and his hair that always had that mussed, sexy look. And of course he wore nothing but shorts. So distracting to her senses. It didn't matter that she knew every line of muscle by heart. She chewed on the end of her pencil while she studied him.

"I have a dinner with business associates tomorrow night. Come with me," he said as he got up out of his chair and knelt down in front of her. He took the pad and pencil out of her hands and pushed her back so his mouth skimmed along her stomach.

She clenched her hands in his hair and gave him what they both wanted. She never answered him, but she didn't have to. The countdown clock was too loud, and she planned to spend every moment she could with him.

THE NEXT EVENING, she got ready in her room. She wanted to surprise him. She could only guess the type of people he worked with, but she bet sophisticated would be a good description. So her makeup was subdued, but there. Her lips shiny, but not red, and her little black dress matched her black heels. She turned and looked in the mirror over her shoulder. Makeup hid the tattoo on her shoulder.

She met him at his door.

He smiled, placed a kiss just under her ear, and they went to Vortex Lounge, which was reserved for guests in the Grand Suites only. It was located on the same deck as his room. As soon as they stepped inside, she wanted to turn right back around and leave. It didn't help when Cole frowned and touched her shoulder where her tattoo was hidden. Luckily, he didn't say anything.

The people standing around looked as haughty as the tailored clothes they wore. The hostess sniffed at her, but smiled at Cole as they were led a group of five other individuals. Introductions were made and they sat. She tried to keep her stomach from cramping, but it was obvious she wasn't welcome. The women glared, the men stripped her, and even though Cole's arm was draped over the back of her chair, they never let up. Not a one of them tried to include her in the conversation.

Cole knew them by name and talked with them easily. She figured out he'd known these people for years. Especially the couple he was designing the house for.

She did not fit.

She excused herself to go to the restroom, any reason to gather her wits. Her heart squeezed painfully as reality sunk in. They hadn't said a word about a future past this cruise, and now she knew why. She looked up into the mirror, wiped away a stray tear and squared her shoulders. She had hoped for a fling, but she'd gotten way more.

She stepped out of the restroom and Cole was waiting for her, fury marking his features.

"We are leaving," he said and led her out of the restaurant and to his room. Once there, he paced back and forth, his hands laced behind his neck.

She crossed her arms over her stomach and waited for it. She knew what was coming. Fighting tears and nausea, she closed her eyes.

"Why did you cover your tattoo?"

She jerked her head in surprise. That wasn't what she expected to hear. "I guessed what type of people would be there."

He strode over to her and dragged her to the bathroom. With a wet towel and none too easy scrubbing, he washed away the makeup. She stared at his hard face in the mirror and said nothing.

"Never hide who you are." His tortured eyes met hers in the mirror.

"Cole, did they say something?"

He dropped the wet rag and hastily left the room. She turned to follow him.

"Ted said I shouldn't bring a dalliance to a business meeting. He said he saw the attraction, but you were no Melanie."

And there it was.

She stumbled back against the wall. Air strangled her. She squeezed her eyes shut. She couldn't watch him say the words. Fuck, what was wrong with her? She should get mad. Storm at him, but it was all she could do to stay on her feet.

"I told him he was right. You weren't Melanie… you're better."

Her eyes popped open in shock. He was pacing again, not looking at her. Pain etched his face and his breath came in harsh puffs.

"There is something I haven't told you." He dropped his hands limply to his sides and looked up. "Melanie was pregnant when she died in the car crash."

That wave of information crushed her and she sagged against the wall. He swallowed and rubbed his palms on the dress slacks that draped his hips so well.

"But there is more. Something I've never told

anyone. Not even my family." He glanced at the ceiling like he was looking for guidance, then back at her. "The baby wasn't mine."

Her mouth dropped open.

"We had been having problems. Hadn't been intimate in a long time. Then she told me she was pregnant. I had no clue she was cheating on me until that moment. She begged me to let her tell everyone. I was so overwhelmed, we'd known each other so long, I agreed. She packed up her stuff, was going to move into *his* home. But she kept putting off telling everyone."

His hands shook and she desperately wanted to go to him. His wife died two years ago. He'd kept this locked up for all that time… only to open up to her. She couldn't even grasp it.

"I was tired of waiting. She was six months along and she was dragging her feet. She didn't know how to tell her parents, but I couldn't do it anymore. I couldn't put on the fake smile and pretend anymore. It was snowing and I told her to stay home, but she was going to *him*." He ran a shaking hand down his face and slumped on the couch. His head fell forward. "She died. Took the secret with her."

She stumbled over to him, knelt on the floor, and took his hands. "Cole."

His hands tightened on hers and his glassy brown eyes stared at her. "I didn't understand why she would do that. Why she would turn to someone else. She'd tried to tell me but I didn't understand. But… I think I get it now."

She flinched away, but he gathered her up and pulled her over his lap, his arm snug around her waist. There were no words. No thought that could follow his thinking.

"This pull we have. All these extremes you make me feel." His knuckle grazed her face. "The need I have for you. It wasn't there with her… or anyone else. Since the moment you shook my hand it's been there. Shouldn't a relationship be more than just comfortable?"

She hadn't even wrapped her head around the word 'relationship' when his thumb brushed along her bottom lip.

"If you could see how your eyes darken when I touch you. I know you feel what I feel." His mouth kissed up her neck, and how much he wanted her was firm and hard against her ass. "This is what has been missing. *You* are what's been missing from my life."

Her heart constricted with his words, and she was lost. This beautiful man saw her but she couldn't keep him. It wouldn't be fair to him.

But she didn't stop him when he pushed her back and pinned her to the couch. He jerked down her shirt and his mouth latched hard onto her nipple. She gasped and arched against him. He pushed up her tight skirt so it bunched around her hips, and ripped at her panties. He snapped open his slacks while she pulled hard at his shirt. The need to feel his bare skin was overwhelming. He helped her shove it off his shoulders, and then his mouth hovered over hers.

"I need you. But we don't fit," she panted against his lips.

"We fit perfectly, *Anjinho Anjo.*" He drove in hard, as though to prove his point.

MUCH LATER, ANGEL lay in his bed, memorizing his sleeping face as tears seeped into her pillow. No matter what he'd said, they weren't a perfect fit, and she wouldn't be the one to hold him back. She didn't fit into his world. Couldn't fit in his world. No matter their connection.

She sucked in her bottom lip, forced herself not to touch him one last time, and quietly got up. She'd gathered her things the day before, so all her stuff was in one place.

She laid the tiny pink shell they'd found on their first outing next to his laptop. It would be up to him to see it.

At the last minute, she grabbed the button down shirt he'd worn the night before and stuffed it in her bag before she slipped out the door, off the boat and to her flight.

CHAPTER EIGHT

COLE STOOD ON the sidewalk and thought about his Angel. The one who'd captured his heart and left it in pieces. Left him with no word. Again. He turned the shell over and over in his fingers. Small yet significant she'd said. So was she.

He stepped into Booseys. It was just as she described. Wooden floors, brick walls, bar on the left, and a stage in the back. Determination in his steps, he stopped at the bar, and looked for his girl. The one he hadn't seen in over a month. Instead, a tiny redhead stopped in front of him.

"What can I get ya?"

He smiled at who he knew to be Lila. "Angel."

She stopped and her bright blue eyes widened. "Holy shit, you're Cole."

He shifted his gaze behind the bar to a tall man with a long goatee. He flung a towel over his shoulder and scowled. "Did you say Angel?"

"Yes, sir. You must be Mick."

Mick widened his stance and crossed his arms over his chest. Cole could see how that would scare some, but he had no intention of leaving without seeing Angel.

"I'm Cole. I met your daughter on the cruise."

They had drawn a crowd now. He recognized each person who was important to her. All the DirtSlap band members along with Cassie and Shelby.

"Why are you here?" Mick asked, his stare never wavering.

"Well, duh. He's here for Angel." Lila's huff interrupted them, then she eyed him up and down. "Damn, she did good."

He chuckled and Lila winked at him. "Don't worry. She didn't tell me much. She's very private but I caught her more than once looking at your picture on her phone. Why the hell did it take you so long?"

"That's a great question," Mick said.

"If it's all the same to you, I'd rather tell her first. Is she here?"

Mick raised a dark brow. "No. She's not. So tell me."

"I mean no disrespect, but I think it's something she needs to hear first."

"The dude has balls, I'll give him that," Cassie said and smirked.

"I'll take that as a compliment, Cassie." Her green eyes widened and he met each shocked gaze. "Yes, I know who each and every one of you are and I'd love to talk, but I need to see Angel. Can someone tell me where I can find her?"

IT WASN'T LONG and he had her address, thanks to Lila who had hastily written it down and shoved him out the door.

He'd been furious when he'd woken up alone on the boat. Everything he'd poured out to her and she'd disappeared without a word. All it took was two weeks away from her, being with his family, seeing the people he associated with and knowing they were the same as those people at their last dinner. All of them knew Melanie. No one there would accept her. His family would, but not his business associates.

So he'd come clean with his parents. Shipped all of Melanie's stuff to her parents and put his house up for sale, furniture and all. Kept only his personal belongings, hopped in his truck, and headed to Nashville.

Now he stood at her door.

Alien Ant Farm blared from her loft apartment. He knocked, and when nothing happened, he banged louder. The music fell down a notch, and she yanked open the door.

He'd been starved for her, and there she stood, wearing his button down shirt, a bandana tied up in her hair, and a paintbrush in her hand. The lips he'd missed parted, the paintbrush fell to the floor, a tear slid down her face, and she launched at him.

He staggered back a step as he caught her. Her arms tight around his neck, her legs around his waist, she buried her face in his neck.

He inhaled her scent and pulled the bandana from her black hair so he could shove his hands in it. With his heart beating double time, he stepped into her home and kicked the door shut behind him. He hadn't known what to expect, since she disappeared without a goodbye. He had prepared a speech, had arguments laid out to convince her they belonged together—then hungry lips sought his.

ANGEL CLUNG TO him. He was here... he was really here. God, she needed him. She slanted her lips over his and he answered. A month and a half without him had been an eternity. She didn't care why he was here, only that he was, and she needed him. Frantic, her hands clawed at his back, pulling at his t-shirt. They fell on her bed and she rolled him, breaking the kiss to yank his shirt off.

He felt too real to be a dream, and she wasn't wasting a moment to figure out if he was or not. His skin was hot, his warm eyes luring her in. She unsnapped his shorts, and with her legs braced on either side of his hips, she slammed him in.

"Cole," she panted.

He sat up and cupped her face, his breath heavy on her cheek. "You're wearing my shirt."

She whimpered, wanting to move, needing him to move. He took his time, unbuttoning the shirt, while he filled and pulsed within her. She bit his lip as she quickly flung the shirt away. He rolled, grabbed her hands, pinned them above her head, and moved. Oh, how he moved. Every nerve alive. Every ache filled with all he could give. Every broken piece of her heart mended.

"Anjinho Anjo, coracao. Eu te amo."

Her eyes flew open. His voice was a balm on her soul, even if she didn't understand the words. The reverence was there. His nose brushed along her cheek.

"Little Angel, my heart. I love you."

Tears slipped down her face as she arched into every stroke. She clung to him as he buried his head against her and came, filling her. She cried out, her legs and arms wrapped tight around him.

He lifted his head and wiped at her tears.

"You left me," he murmured with pain in his eyes. "Why?"

With their bodies still joined, he wanted to talk? "I… we… we don't fit. Our worlds—"

"Fit." His thumb traced her lower lip like he always had before, and she closed her eyes because she'd missed it so much. "I sold my house. Turned over that branch of my business to my brother

Adam. I can start another branch anywhere. Anywhere you want to live. Here or anywhere."

She gaped at him and her heart skipped a beat, then hammered in her chest. "You sold your house? You loved that house."

He shook his head and a slow smile spread across his face. "I can build another house. One that fits us."

"Us?"

"I'm not letting you go again. I love you, Angel."

She trailed her fingers along his face and he kissed her palm. "I love you, too."

A grin split his face. "I know you do."

She blinked, then burst out laughing.

"Ah my Angel, you know what your laugh does to me." He nuzzled her neck and she turned her face toward him.

"How did you find me anyway?"

He arched a brow and smirked. "Lila."

She laughed again as they rolled across the bed.

KRUSH is a novella and #3 in the DirtSlap Series.

FUEL DirtSlap Series #1 is Cassie and Thrand's story.

WRECK DirtSlap Series #2 is Ethan and Shelby's story.

Both available now at all major retailers.

Two more DirtSlap novels are coming soon.

Ashlynn Pearce

Were it not for Hope, the Heart would Break…

Once upon a time… *You ain't gonna believe this shit!*

(I always wanted to start a bio like that!) But seriously—scrap that, I'm not serious, but I do love to write. Create characters. Give them hope that there is something better around the corner. It's my passion. I live and breathe stories. When I'm not arguing with the characters in my head (yes, I do that, you can ask my hubby who thinks I'm nuts btw), I'm taking care of said hubby, my two kids and a melee of furbabies. I'm Okie born and bred and, yes, we get a lot of twisters and, no, there aren't any teepees around that I've seen.

Come on over, say hi and see what I'm up to!

www.AshlynnPearce.com
FB: www.facebook.com/ashlynnpearcewriter
Twitter: @Ashlynn_Pearce

Made in the USA
Coppell, TX
13 July 2026

84130809R00059